SAFARI CIRCUS

FUN WITH THE ANIMAL STARS

D1260975

Akash Pandya

The elephant moves
with grace and might,
stomping and swaying,
a majestic sight.

Moose joins the party, ready to play. Tapping his hooves, in a rhythmic display.

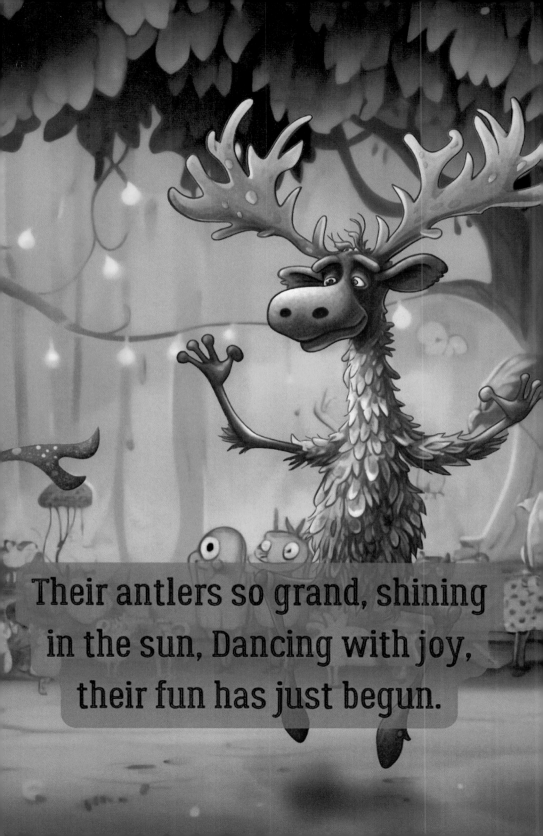

Their antlers so grand, shining
in the sun, Dancing with joy,
their fun has just begun.

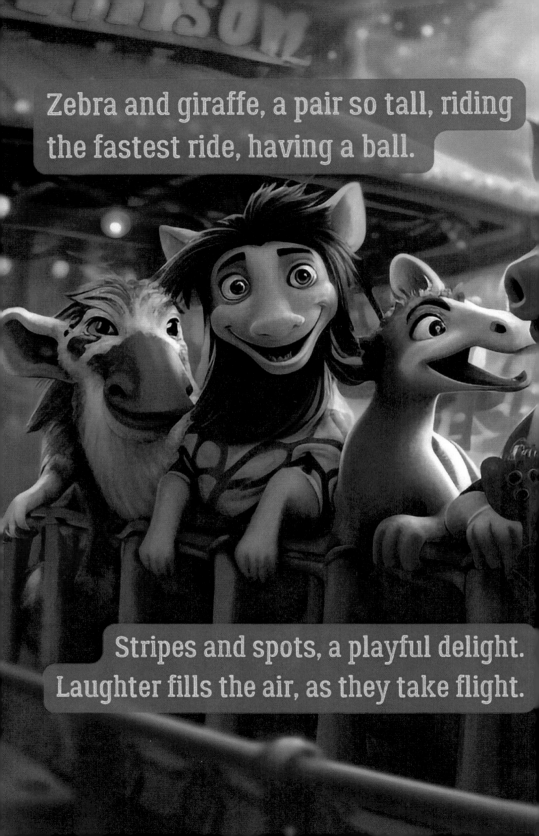

Zebra and giraffe, a pair so tall, riding the fastest ride, having a ball.

Stripes and spots, a playful delight. Laughter fills the air, as they take flight.

SAFARI CIRCUS

FUN WITH THE ANIMAL STARS

Their musical talents, a sight to behold,
As they entertain with songs, both new and old.

The jungle comes alive with their joyous sound, As the baby monkeys' concert echoes all around.

So join the frogs, in their hop and their bound, Let their dance and ribbits fill the surround.

Snow leopard sings, a voice pure and clear. Melting hearts with each note, drawing near. Bringing warmth and joy, like a born 🔥 **fire**.

Parrot strums the guitar, feathers in a blaze, melodies soar, capturing hearts in a daze. Crowds gather 'round, to hear the sweet sound, his tunes enchanting, all the way around.

Owl the comedian, a hoot so grand, Making the jungle laugh, as he takes a stand.

With feathers ruffled and a cheeky flair, He fills the air with laughter, beyond compare.

Swan rides a bike, graceful and grand, Performing tricks, all across the land.

Bull steps up on stage, his cape in hand,
magic tricks aplenty, he'll make you understand.

With a wave and a flick, illusions unfold,
Gasps of wonder, his secrets never sold.

showing off stunts, thrilling me and you.

Dolphin dives and splashes, in the water so blue

So if you ever spot, a group of rabbits so fine, with blue eyes shining, as they intertwine,

Watch them breakdance, with skill and grace,
A performance that'll put a smile on your face.

So if you're in the jungle, keep your eyes open wide, For the chimp on his bike, going on a wild ride.

He's the gravity-defying star, with skills so grand, A fearless performer, in the jungle's great land.

Made in United States
North Haven, CT
23 July 2023

39428785R00015